THE DOODLES STRIKE BACK

Written and illustrated by
Zack Giallongo

EGMONT
We bring stories to life

First published in Great Britain 2017
by Egmont UK Limited, The Yellow Building,
1 Nicholas Road, London W11 4AN.

Edited by Craig Jelley
Design and colour by Maddox Philpot

ISBN 978 1 4052 8512 4
65808/1
Printed in Poland

Stay safe online. Egmont is not responsible for content hosted by third parties.

To find more great Star Wars books, visit www.egmont.co.uk/starwars

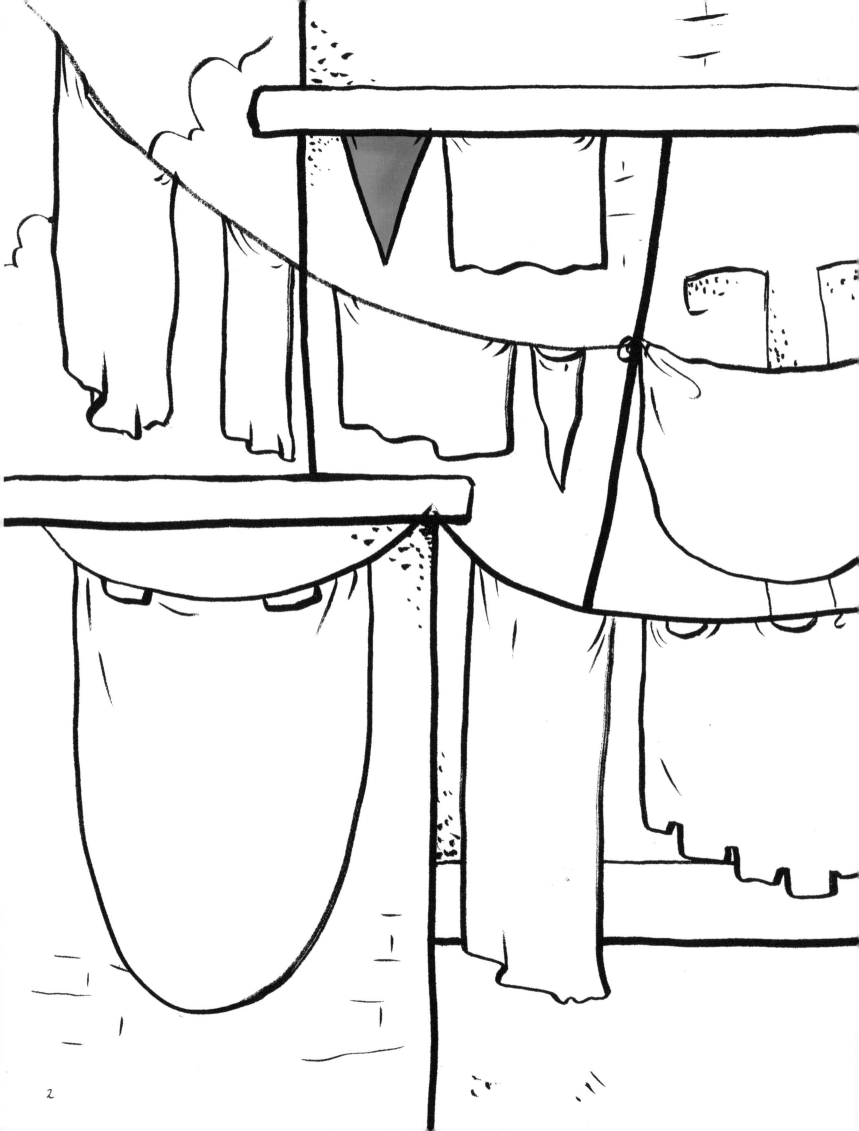

Design some cool banners
for Maz's castle!

Rey is tired of eating crummy food.
Draw her something delicious to eat.

FWOOSH! What's shooting out of the flametrooper's flamethrower?

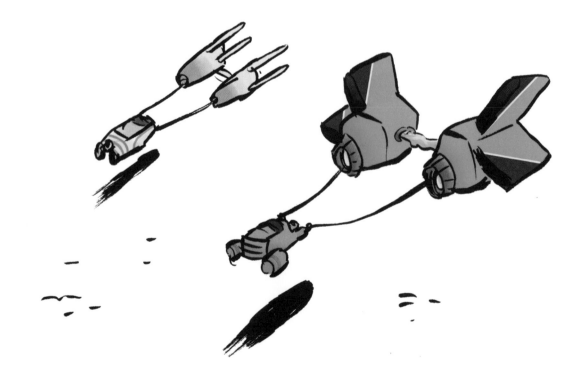

Draw some obstacles for the podracers to avoid.

Why not design a new jacket for Poe?

Colour in Captain Phasma's cape and use stars to show how shiny and polished her armour is.

Help Rey through the maze
to find Master Luke.

START

Darth Maul is already scary, but can you make him scarier by designing new face markings?

Hux just needs a friend. Draw one for him!

Oh, no! What are Anakin and Obi-Wan
facing in the arena of Geonosis?

The rest of these
Twi'leks need
lekku like Hera's.
Draw them on.

Draw the Jedi who sliced through this battle droid.

Count Dooku is trying out some new beard styles. Help him out!

Finn is so thirsty in the Jakku desert. Draw him a tasty beverage.

Draw an ace rebel pilot in this X-wing.

Maz Kanata's eyes are very unusual,
don't you agree? Draw them in!

Give this Wookiee warrior a cool fur pattern.

Kylo Ren is deep in thought on Starkiller Base, but what is he thinking about?

Draw some weird wares for Watto to sell in his workshop.

It's fully operational! Use squiggles, lines and dots to draw a blast coming from the Death Star.

Time to give your old pal Ziro
the Hutt a new design on his body.

What new attachments do Thromba
and Laparo have on their arms?

Who has arrived on the *Falcon* to keep lonely Luke company?

Decorate this clone trooper's helmet.

What kind of creature are Wicket and Teebo hunting down?

What colour are these younglings' lightsabers?

Draw stripes on
Ahsoka's lekku!

Use different shapes to draw armour
on the luggabeast.

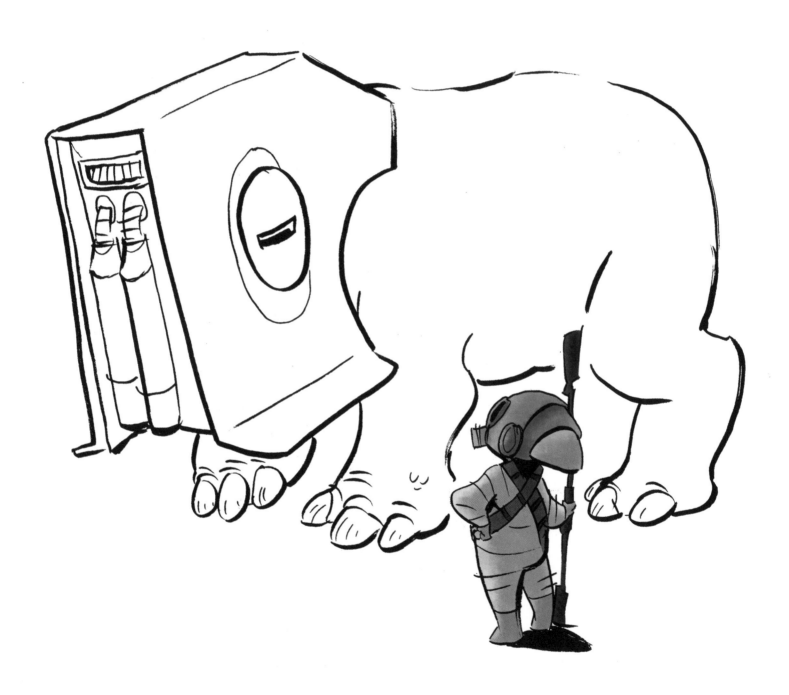

Waaargh! What's chasing after Jar Jar?
Draw something scary.

What is Rey salvaging from
this old, busted ship?

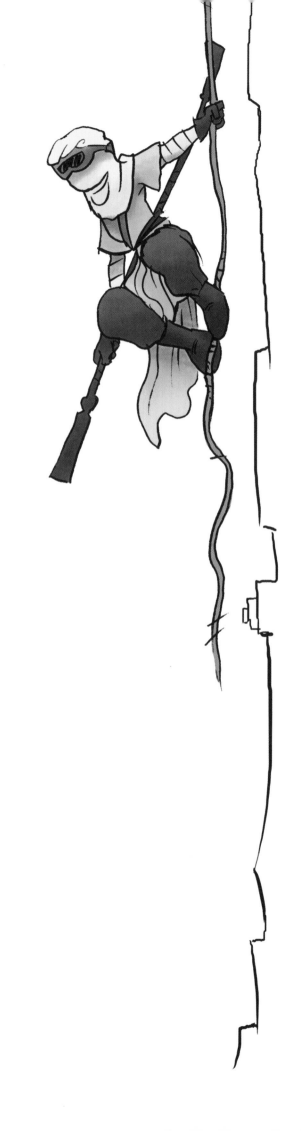

General Grievous has four missing arms.
Draw them in!

Who, or what, is joining the happabore for a drink at Niima Outpost?

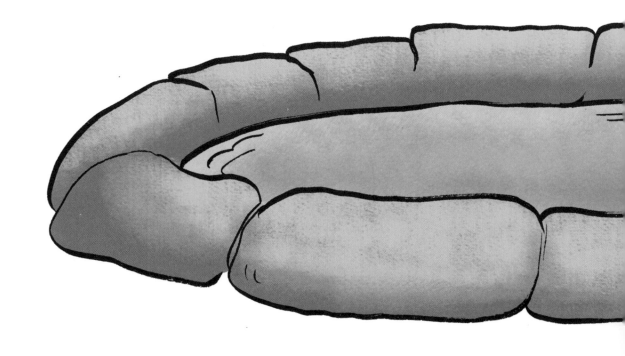

Lightsabers don't normally look like that! What's different about Ezra's new lightsaber?

That was close! Who are Finn and Poe hiding from?

Temper, temper! What did Kylo Ren destroy this time?

Sabine has some rad new colours in
her hair, and cool new armour to match.

What luggage is HURID-327 carrying around Maz's castle?

What does General Organa see on her screen?

Cover this dewback
in scaly skin!

What do Luke and Biggs
see up in the sky?

Draw some jets blasting out of Chopper.

Draw the slimy space slug that lives in this meteor.

Draw your favourite food
to feed to the rancor!

Who are Sidon and Quiggold interviewing to join their crew?

Uh-oh! Quick! Draw something for Ahsoka to land on.

Use lines and squiggles to show
Mace Windu's Force push.

Give Amidala's reek some cool
warpaint as it thunders into battle.

Draw tentacles on the rathtar.

Who else does it have in its grasp?

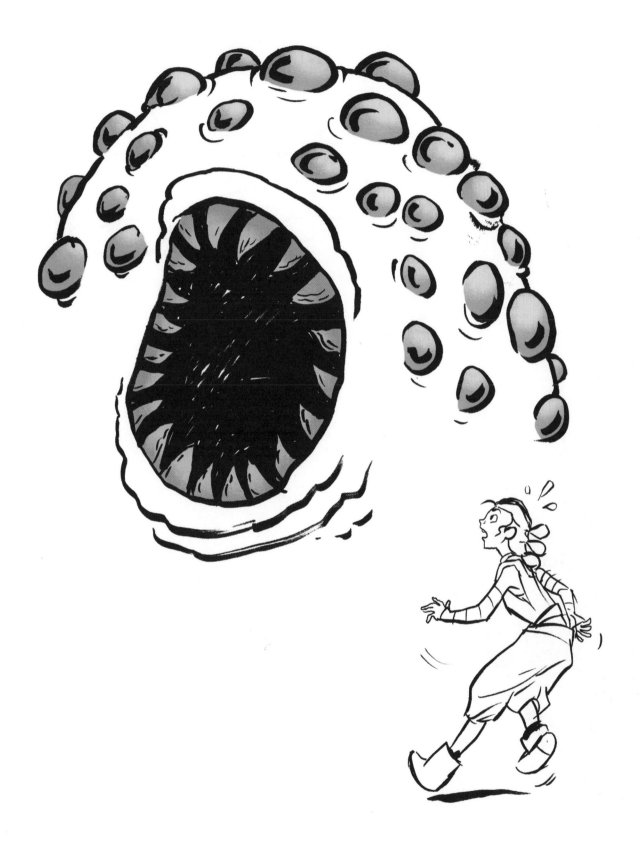

BOOM! What's Chewie shooting at? Draw blaster fire coming from his bowcaster too.

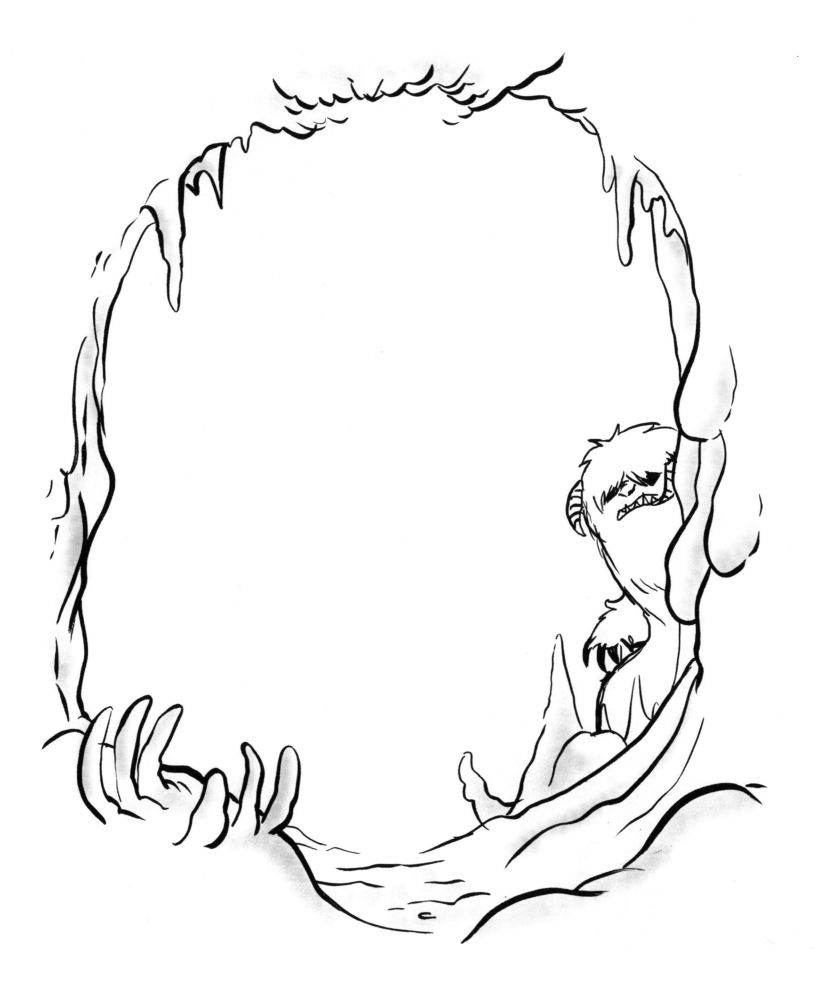

What is hanging up in the wampa's cave?

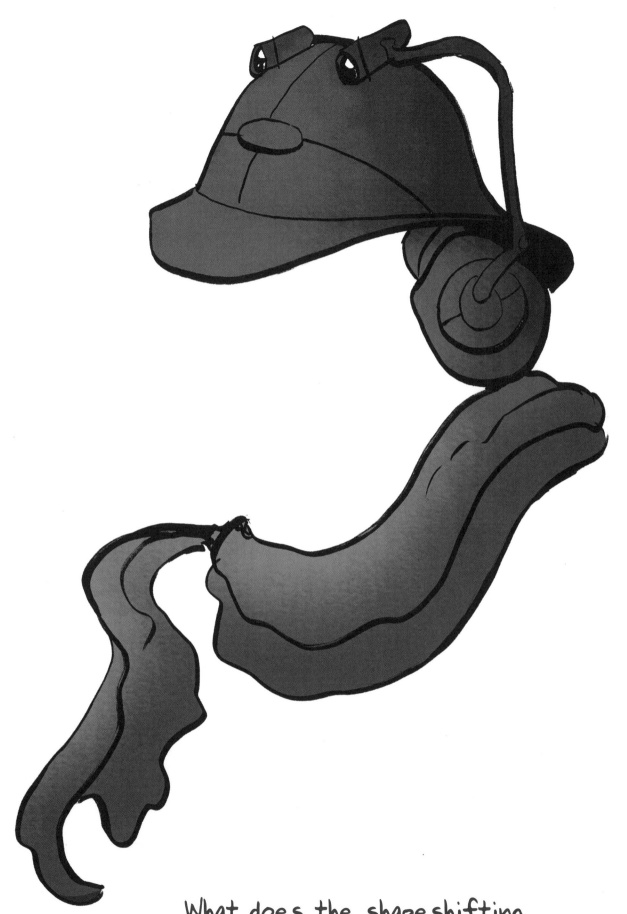

What does the shapeshifting assassin Zam Wesell look like today?

Use circles and squares to draw a
compressor for Rey to bypass.

Give BB-8 a fresh coat of paint,
and add in his flame.

What do Darth Maul's
new legs look like?

Give these clone troopers some cool hairstyles.

Help Snap Wexley decorate his droid.

Who is at the end of Jabba's chain?

KA-POW! Draw ships battling over Coruscant.

Draw the alien customer that Maz is serving.

Use lines and squiggles to fill
Zeb's fur with new stripes.

Logray is weaving a spell for these young woklings.
What does it look like?

Oh no! Vader stole Han's blaster. Quickly draw him something new!

Use different shapes to draw
Unkar Plutt's armour.

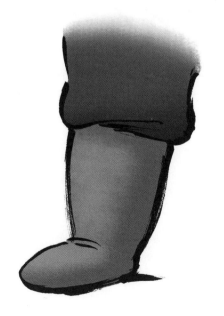

Customise the Millennium Falcon
with some cool new features.

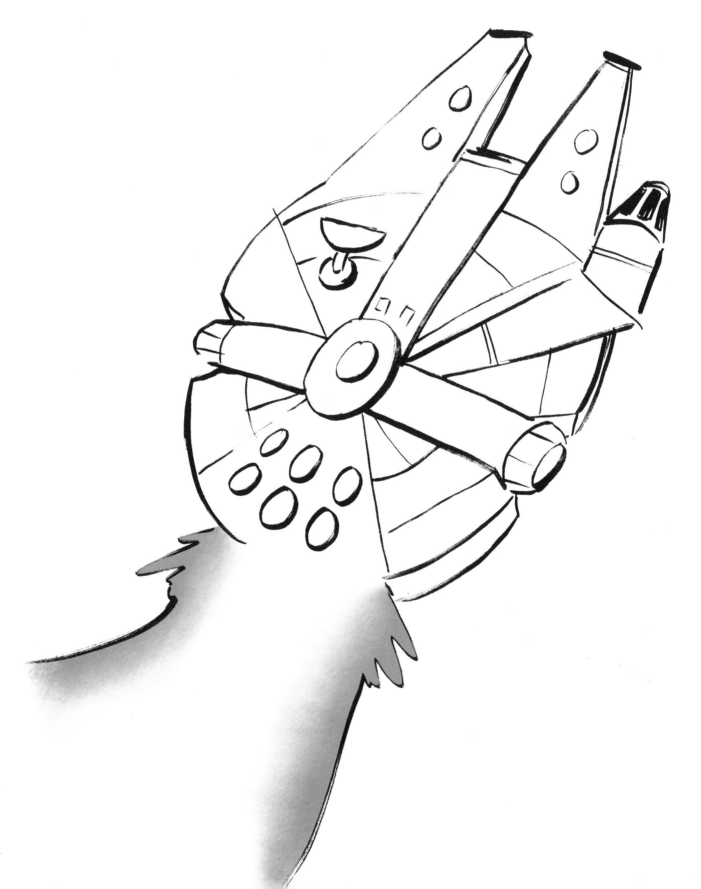

What weird ingredients is
Aunt Beru putting in the soup?

Han is trying to talk his way out of a situation again, but which menacing character is he in trouble with?

Give Queen Amidala some new make-up.

Rey and Kylo Ren are about to battle! Draw a lightsaber for each and an epic Starkiller Base backdrop.

How many musical notes can you draw around Sy Snootles?

What are these Jawas stealing?

Draw bridges, ropes
and ladders so the
Ewoks can get around.

Give this wampa some scary horns!

Draw these senators something to sit on.

Draw lava, flames and ash on Mustafar.

There's a storm brewing!
Draw a sandstorm ripping
across Tatooine.

Add some tall grass for these tookas
and tiny creatures for them to hunt.

Ol' Rex has seen a lot of battle. What kind of trophies does he have on his wall?

HELP! Draw a hero to pull
C-3PO out of the Dune Sea.

Something is stalking Luke on his tauntaun. What is it?

Sebulba drives dirty. Draw the items
that he's throwing at his opponents.

Who, or what, are the Kaminoans cloning in these chambers?

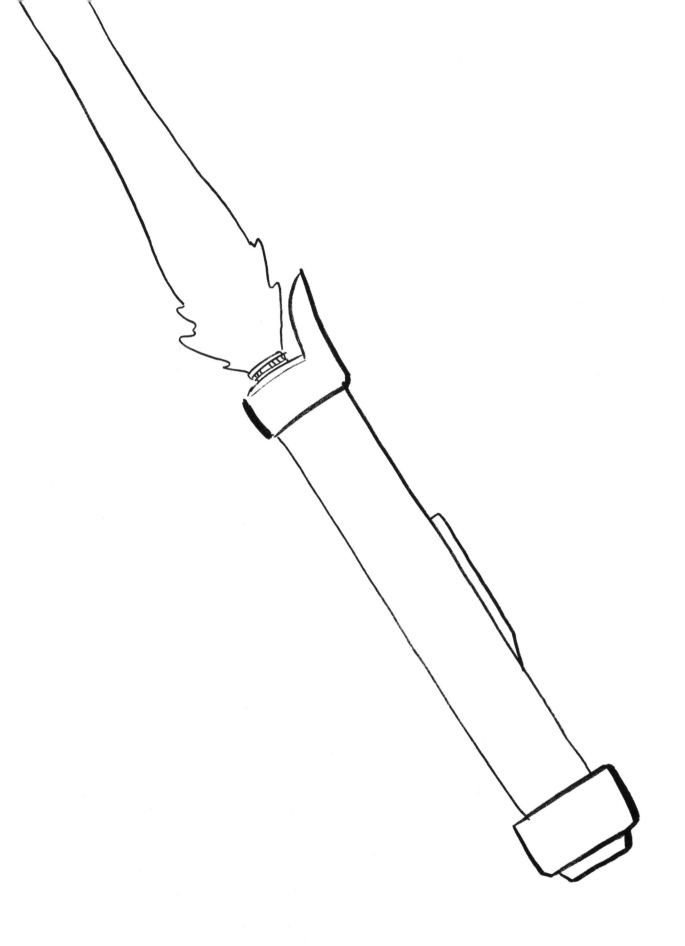

Design this lightsaber handle. Add lots of different shapes to the hilt to make it look cool!

Help colour the camouflage on Leia's poncho.

The Jawa sandcrawler lost its treads.
Draw it some new wheels!

Lounging about will not be tolerated!
What did Vader catch the stormtroopers doing?

What's the best tool R2-D2 can use
to get free from the Ewoks' trap?

Use boxes to draw Snoke's throne.

Give Ki-Adi Mundi a humongous hat.

What sort of ears does a gundark have?

Wicket sure could use a new weapon right about now!

Draw what you think a Tusken Raider
might look like under his mask.

Draw a regal pattern on
Senator Palpatine's robes.

What does Maz have in her treasure chest?

Which sinister person is addressing the First Order?

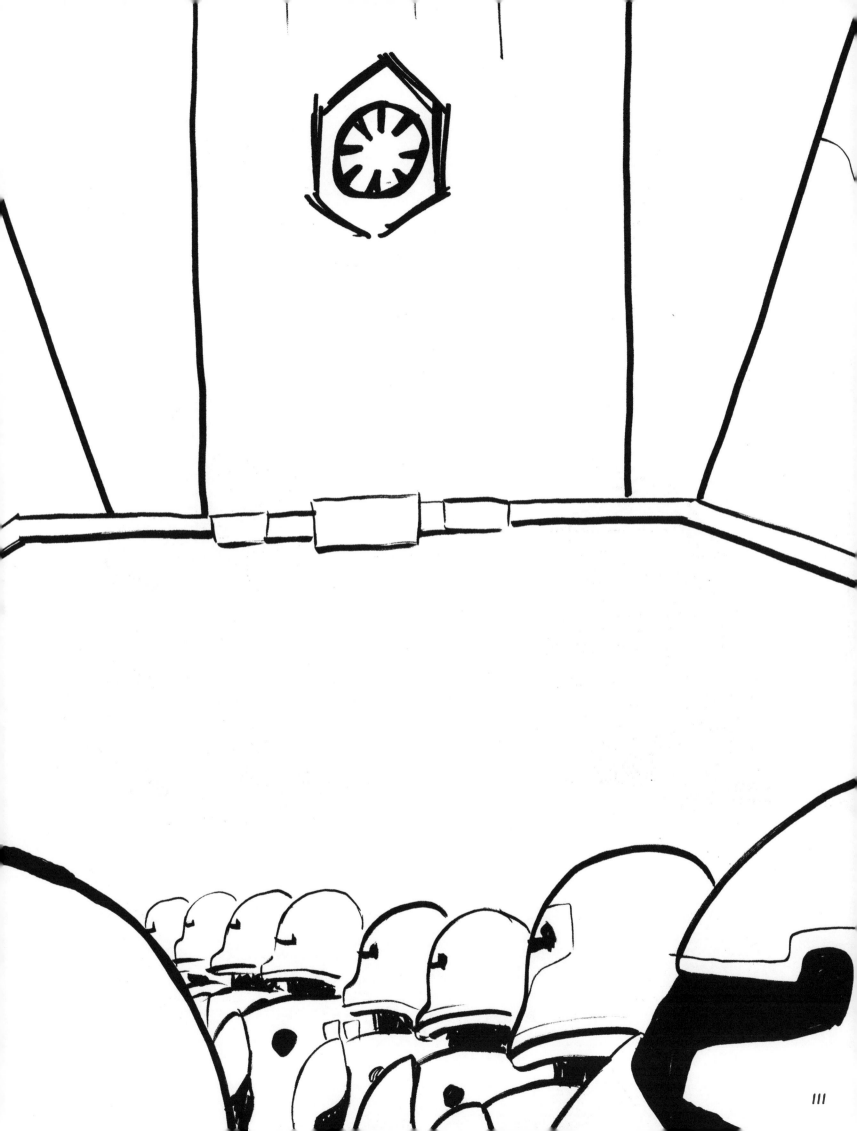

Now that AP-5 and Chopper are pals,
what game are they playing?

Stinky is being a brat. Draw Ahsoka
a toy to calm him down.

Whoops! What did the AT-ST accidentally step on?

What kind of wings do mynocks have?

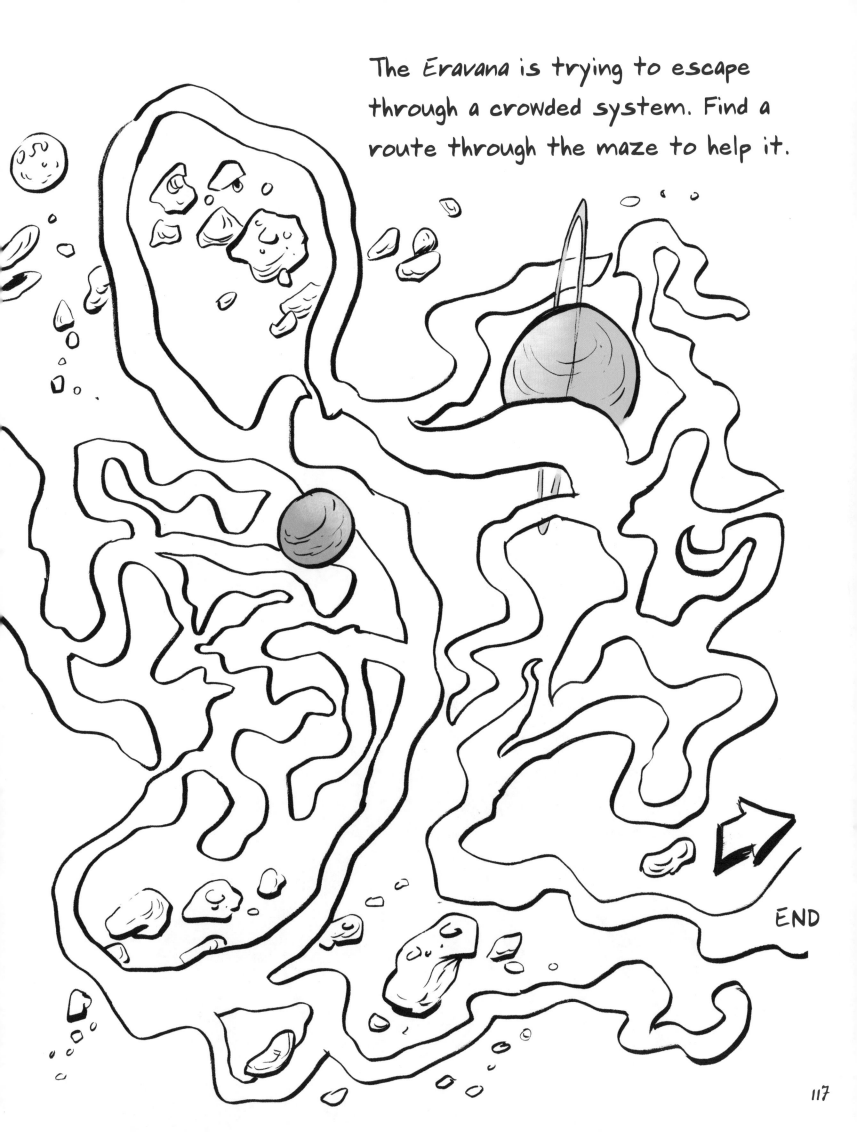

The *Eravana* is trying to escape through a crowded system. Find a route through the maze to help it.

END

Design some new blasters for Rey and Finn.

Amidala's handmaiden is rescuing
her from a huge explosion. Draw it!

Draw the bloodsucking insects of Dagobah.

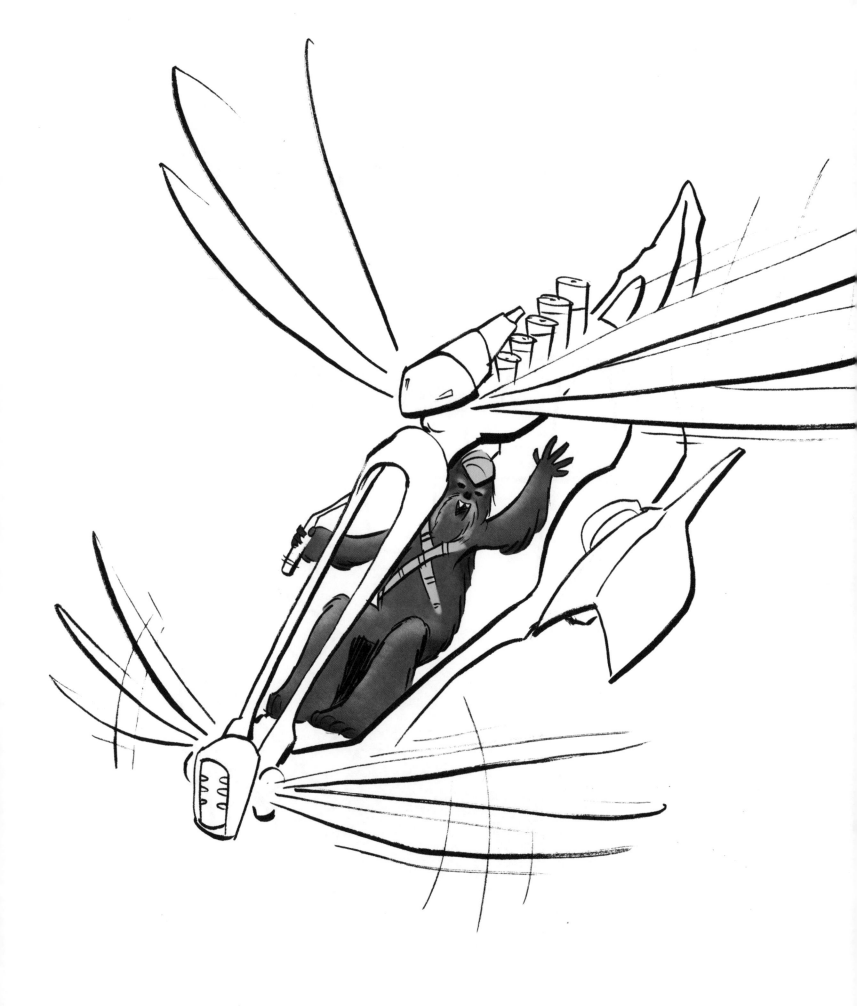

Decorate this Wookiee catamaran!

What crazy creatures is Bobbajo carrying in his cages?

Hondo Ohnaka is hunting for treasure.
What riches is he about to get his hands on?

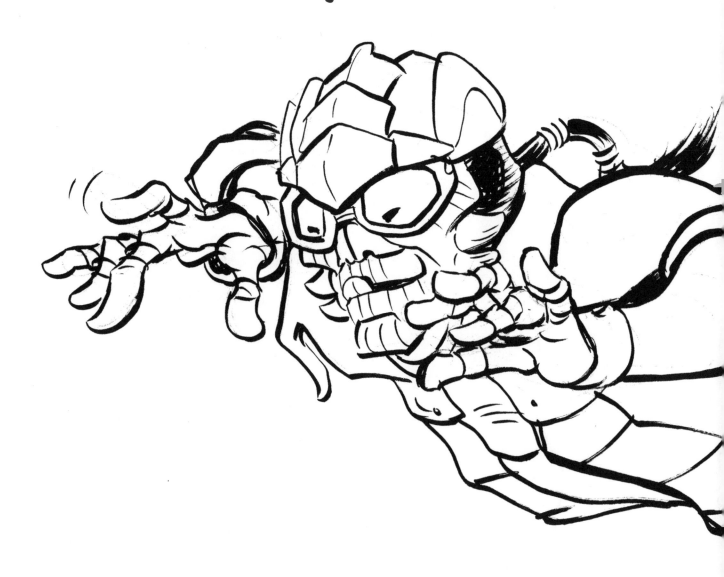

What have R2-D2 and
C-3PO found in this cave?

Yoda can't tackle Darth Bane alone this time. Draw him some Jedi friends to help him win the battle

Use lines to show Lux the way to Ahsoka.